A Different Game

A Different Game

Sylvia Olsen

ORCA BOOK PUBLISHERS

Library and Archives Canada Cataloguing in Publication

Olsen, Sylvia, 1955-
A different game / written by Sylvia Olsen.
(Orca young readers)

ISBN 978-1-55469-169-2

I. Title. II. Series: Orca young readers
PS8579.L728D53 2010   JC813'.6   C2009-906856-7

First published in the United States, 2010
Library of Congress Control Number: 2009940906

Summary: In this sequel to *Murphy and Mousetrap*, Murphy and his three friends
are nervous about trying out for the soccer team at their new school, but a diagnosis
of leukemia proves more challenging than anything they encounter on the field.

Mixed Sources
Product group from well-managed forests,
controlled sources and recycled wood or fiber
www.fsc.org   Cert no. SW-COC-000952
FSC   © 1996 Forest Stewardship Council

*Orca Book Publishers is dedicated to preserving the environment and has printed this book on paper
certified by the Forest Stewardship Council.*

Orca Book Publishers gratefully acknowledges the support for its publishing programs provided
by the following agencies: the Government of Canada through the Canada Book Fund
and the Canada Council for the Arts, and the Province of British Columbia through
the BC Arts Council and the Book Publishing Tax Credit.

Typesetting by Bruce Collins
Cover artwork by Ken Dewar
Author photo by Rob Campbell Photography

The building and totem poles pictured on the cover of *A Different Game* are artist's renderings of
Tseshaht structures and totems in Port Alberni, British Columbia.

ORCA BOOK PUBLISHERS   ORCA BOOK PUBLISHERS
PO Box 5626, Stn. B   PO Box 468
Victoria, BC Canada   Custer, WA USA
V8R 6S4   98240-0468

www.orcabook.com
Printed and bound in Canada.

13 12 11 10   •   5 4 3 2

Dedicated to Amory,
who played a different game and won

Chapter One

Murphy gets to the field late. The other boys are already there—all three of them. He joins their huddle near the bleachers, catching his breath.

"It's about time," Albert says. He slaps Murphy on the back.

"Yeah, Murph, we've been waiting for you," Jeff says. He leans into the circle and frowns at Murphy. Jeff is serious about everything. But he's not the only one who's serious about soccer. Murphy hadn't meant to be late. It's just that Mom makes him do chores before he plays in the morning. "We've got to practice hard," Jeff continues. "We're going to show Riverside Middle School that the best soccer players come from the Long Inlet Tribal School."

Albert pounds his chest. "They ain't seen nothing yet," he says. "All four of us are going to make the team."

Murphy is excited about going to middle school. Especially about trying out for the soccer team. But deep inside he has a few niggling fears. He liked the Long Inlet Tribal School, even though he'd only been there for one year. He knew everyone at the school. Half of them were related to him. He liked the way Mom came to the school and helped make lunch for all the kids. They always had great stuff like tacos and spaghetti.

At Riverside, Murphy will have to get up early and catch a bus—every morning. And Jeff, Albert and Danny are the only three guys he will know at the new school. There will be at least a couple of hundred kids who will be complete strangers. Mom says once he gets to middle school he'll be making his own lunch in the morning, so he better get used to eating sandwiches. Murphy doesn't like the sound of that at all.

When it comes right down to it, the only thing Murphy likes about going to Riverside is the soccer team. And then again, that is the worst problem of all.

The boys from the tribal school are at a big disadvantage, and Murphy knows it. First of all, they're only in grade seven and most of the middle-school team are going to be in grade eight. Second of all, the other grade sevens trying out for the team will already have been in the school. The coach already knows them; he'll surely pick a kid he knows over one from the tribal school.

"Uncle Rudy says we're the best grade-seven players ever to go to Riverside," Jeff says.

"Let's hear it for Uncle!" Albert high-steps and slaps his knees. Murphy doesn't think Rudy is Jeff's uncle, but on the reserve everyone seems to be related to one another. It's easier just to call any older man Uncle and any older woman Auntie; that way you don't offend anyone. "He made the Riverside team, and now he's a soccer superstar. If he can do it, we can do it," says Albert.

Just a couple of years ago, Uncle Rudy played for the Canadian World Cup soccer team, which makes him about the most famous guy ever to come from Long Inlet Reserve. A lot of people, including Murphy, put it down to the fact that he broke into the Riverview lineup in grade seven.

"But that doesn't mean we've got it made," Danny says. "It means we have to show our stuff. Especially if all four of us are going to make the starting lineup."

"Come on then. If we're going to show our stuff, we better get our stuff together," Murphy says. "Cut the talk. Let's do something."

The boys take their spots on the field—Albert at center, Danny at offense, Jeff at defense and Murphy in the goal. They play half a field until Levi and Haywire arrive. It's not long before enough boys show up so they can play five a side.

Most of the boys are only going into grade six, and a few of the others aren't serious soccer players. It's just the four of them—Albert, Danny, Jeff and Murphy—who will be attending Riverside and trying out for the team. That's the reason there's a soccer game every day throughout the summer—to get ready. Younger boys and even non-soccer players come out to help prepare the grade sevens for the September tryouts. It's been a Long Inlet tradition ever since Uncle Rudy made the team.

Sometimes one player from the reserve gets picked for the Riverside starting lineup, rarely two, but never four. But like Uncle Rudy says, there's never been such a pool of Long Inlet grade-seven talent heading to middle school.

"You go, Albert," Haywire shouts. "You're the best since Uncle Rudy. Riverside's not going to know what hit them."

Haywire might be right. Even Uncle Rudy says as much—maybe not right out loud, but it's easy to tell that Uncle Rudy is amazed at Albert's skill. It's no secret. All the boys, and pretty much everyone else on the Long Inlet Reserve, know that Albert is the best young soccer player they have ever seen.

Levi passes to Albert. Albert takes the ball as if he's got a magnet in his foot. He dribbles it around Haywire like the guy is standing still. He dekes around Jeff, making him look like he's sitting on his heels, and charges straight for Murphy, who's crouched and ready. Albert aligns his body. At first it looks as if he's going to drill the ball high and directly at Murphy. Murphy's all set—legs bent, eyes on the ball, hands up. Then, at the last split second, Albert shifts his weight, fakes Murphy out and slams the ball into the back of the net.

"Jeez, Murph, where were you?" he shouts, and then he laughs.

Albert runs to Murphy as he's picking up the ball.

"High five," Albert says, bouncing on the balls of his feet.

"Forget it," Murphy says. "You're looking at the starting keeper. Try that again and see how good you are."

Albert dribbles back to center field.

"That won't happen next time," Murphy hollers.

Danny does a four-finger whistle, and the game starts again.

Levi lets a shot go, and Connor tries one, but they don't have a chance. Murphy is good. Really good. He gets in front of the ball, hits it, traps it, blocks it— whatever it takes, Murphy does it. He is on his game, and it feels good. The Riverside coach can't possibly overlook him. But, in the back of his mind, he knows the goalie position is the hardest position to take, especially if the coach already has someone in mind.

"Look out, Murph," Jeff hollers. "Here comes Albert."

This time Albert takes a shot toward the top left-hand corner of the net. He knows it's Murphy's weak spot. For some reason Murphy's left leg has slower reflexes than his right. The whole left side of his body seems to lack the lightning-fast responses that he can count on from his right side.

It's not as if Murphy is slow on his left side—not compared to other boys. But he can feel a slight lag time in his muscles. The only other person who knows about Murphy's right/left difference is Albert. And when Albert knows a player has a weakness, he makes sure he uses that weakness to his advantage.

"Nice try," Albert shouts.

"Nice shot," Murphy shouts back.

Albert is fast, and he's tough. In the winter, when Murphy first started playing soccer with the boys, he thought Albert just blasted his way to being a good player. Bull strength—bigger is better—was what Murphy thought of as Albert's style.

But since the tournament in the spring, when the Long Inlet Buckskins went to Victoria to the Easter tournament—the biggest soccer tournament on the Island—and won the trophy, Murphy has come to know a few other things about Albert: he is smart; his eye doesn't miss a thing; and he plays your weaknesses.

Before the Easter tournament, when Uncle Rudy asked the team what part of the body was most important to a good soccer player, Albert had been the first one to shout an answer. "Muscle," he said, flexing his arms. Danny said legs. Jeff said feet.

"No, think about it," Uncle Rudy said, pointing to his head.

That's when Murphy figured it out. "The brain," he said.

"You got it right, Murph," Uncle Rudy said. "And don't you boys forget it. A soccer player has to use his head first."

But smart wasn't something Murphy would have called Albert. Not until recently. Now Albert is sharp. He watches all the players. He knows what they're good at and what they're not so good at. No matter how hard Murphy tries to compensate for his slower left side, he doesn't fool Albert.

The ball sails right past Murphy. No higher than his head, but just out of reach and faster than he can respond to.

"You go, Albert," Connor hollers.

"Woooowwww, nice shot," Haywire shouts.

"You're going to blow those middle-school coaches away," Jeff says. "Albert Adams, the new starting center for the Riverside Strikers, coming right up."

One more thing about Albert. He inspires other players. He's a hero to younger boys like Haywire. They dream that one day they will play like Albert, but for now they are happy to feed him the ball and cheer him on.

Chapter Two

Wednesday is Uncle Rudy's day off. So by 10:00 AM, he's at the field waiting for the boys to show up.

"How's it been going?" he asks Jeff and Murphy when they arrive at the bleachers. "Have you guys been running? Are you doing the drills I gave you last week? Are you working on your squats?" He points at Murphy.

"Yeah," Murphy says. "Most days."

"Most days aren't good enough, Nephew." Uncle Rudy cuffs Murphy good-naturedly on his shoulder. "Every day. Nothing less than every day. Dedication makes a good athlete."

"Okay, okay," Murphy says.

He knows Uncle Rudy is right, but Murphy would rather play a game than do the exercises. It's the same with the other boys.

"That's why I'm here on Wednesdays," Uncle Rudy says when a few more boys arrive. "It's a workday. Drills, running, drills, running—we are going to make superstars out of each and every one of you."

He matches the boys up in pairs and leads them through agility and ball-handling drills. They do strength exercises and even some yoga. The first time Uncle Rudy had the team do a yoga breathing exercise, the boys laughed at him. But after a few weeks of doing yoga stretches, Murphy could tell the difference. Those weird moves make him feel two inches taller and way more limber.

Uncle Rudy works the boys in small groups and individually. It isn't until after they have a break and eat oranges, which Uncle Rudy always brings, that he leads them in a game.

He makes sure Albert and Murphy are never on the same team. That way Murphy gets to experience trying to save Albert's shots. If it weren't for Albert,

Murphy would never have become such a good goalie. Albert's skills have made Murphy faster, tougher and smarter. And for that he is thankful. And besides, Albert is the only player who works Murphy's left side.

Uncle Rudy runs the sidelines hollering at the boys.

"Think about it, Jeff. Anticipate."

He watches each one of the players.

"Don't just give it to Albert, Connor. Make him work for it."

He doesn't criticize, but Uncle Rudy doesn't believe in praising everyone all the time either.

"Albert, Danny's all over your fancy footwork. Let's see some smooth, solid ball control."

After Rudy blows the whistle, he sits on the bleachers, and the boys gather around on the grass.

"We're making good progress. But I'm not here to blow sunshine in your face. I'm here to push you to get better. You are all good players, and every one of you can get better. It's like the soccer field is on an uphill slope. You are heading up—always, always up. Improving, improving, improving."

The boys nod their heads.

"Come on," Rudy says. "I'm looking for some more enthusiasm. Which one of you wants to stay as good as you are today for the rest of your life?"

Haywire tosses up his hand for a second until everyone starts to laugh at him.

"Really?" Uncle Rudy laughs.

"I want to be better?" Haywire says it like it's a question.

"Right on—you figured it out." Uncle Rudy nods his head. "You are better this week than you were last week, and if you do your drills and run, you'll be even better next week. Carry on like this, and who knows how great you will be in the future."

"Right on."

"We'll do it."

"Yeah."

The boys clap their hands and slap each other on the back.

"You grade sevens only have three weeks before school starts. That means there's not much time to work on your game. I want all you other boys to help them out. This is a team effort. And"—he points his finger at Albert, then Jeff, then Danny, then Murphy—"you and you and you and you are going to make us proud.

You are the best lineup I've seen heading up to Riverside since I was in grade seven."

"Yeah right," Murphy says. "You told us only one guy made the team that year and that was you."

"But I forgot to say I was as good as all four of you put together." Uncle Rudy laughs and then says, "Seriously, you guys, I've got to tell you. I don't think I was as good as any one of you. And that's the truth."

The boys stand up.

"We've got one rule, and what is it?" Uncle Rudy hollers.

"Give 'er all you've got!" the boys shout together.

"And?" Uncle Rudy shouts.

"Get 'er done!" they shout louder.

"What's the rule?" Uncle Rudy hollers again.

"Give 'er all you've got!" the boys reply.

"And?" Uncle Rudy shouts.

"Get 'er done!" everyone shouts in unison.

The boys gather in a huddle and put their hands in the middle like spokes on a wheel and shout:

What's our name? Yeah!
What's our name? Yeah!
Get 'er done and win the game!
Gooooooo, Buckskins!

They head back onto the field and take their places.

"Twenty minutes to show your stuff," Uncle Rudy shouts. He blows the whistle, and the game starts again. "Every play, every minute counts."

The boys are tired and hot. It's been a long practice. But with Uncle Rudy on the sidelines, they all try their best. Especially Murphy. He makes sure no one, not even Albert, gets another goal.

● ● ●

The next three weeks scoot by like they're just a couple of days. Murphy wishes there was more time. He wants to work on some of his moves. Mostly he wants to work on his confidence. He's only been playing soccer for seven months or so, while the other boys have been playing since they could walk. Everyone plays soccer on the reserve. Little kids look like they have soccer balls attached to the ends of their feet. Murphy was more interested in computers right up until he and his mom moved to Long Inlet.

It helps when Uncle Rudy says stuff like, "Don't agonize over the last play, anticipate the next play.

You're the best you've ever been today, and you'll be better tomorrow!"

Sometimes Murphy doesn't understand the words Uncle Rudy uses, so after practice he asks Mom how to spell the words, and then he looks them up on the computer.

Ag-o-nize: to think about something intensely, usually in great detail and for a long time, before making a decision

An-tic-i-pate: to imagine or consider something before it happens and make any necessary preparations or changes

Once Murphy looks up the words, he knows exactly what Uncle Rudy is talking about. That's the thing Murphy likes about Uncle Rudy—he doesn't think things should come easy. He thinks if it's worth having, you should have to work for it.

Uncle Rudy also understands how the boys feel about leaving the tribal school.

He says, "You're going from what you know and what's comfortable to what you don't know and what feels scary. That's okay. That's called growing up. That's called challenging yourself. Without a challenge, you will stagnate."

Stag-nate: to fail to develop, progress or make necessary changes

What Uncle Rudy says makes it easier, but Murphy still feels a little worried about going to Riverside. Especially when it comes to the soccer team.

⚽ ⚽ ⚽

"I think you're ready," Uncle Rudy says on the last Wednesday before school starts. "I know you're ready. I am positive you're ready. I absolutely have no doubt in the world that you guys are ready. You guys are the Formidable Four. Riverside has never seen anything like it."

The Formidable Four. Murphy rolls the words around in his head. *The Formidable Four*. The words sound awesome. All the boys hold their heads up and pump their chests out when Uncle Rudy shouts, "The Formidable Four. Riverside"—Uncle Rudy spreads his hands like he is making a grand announcement—"let me introduce to you the Formidable Four."

His enthusiasm is catching. The younger boys shout, "The Formidable Four! You go, guys!"

All the boys are excited when they stand in a huddle and shout:

> What's our name? Yeah!
> What's our name? Yeah!
> Get 'er done and win the game!
> Goooooo, Riverside!

Saying *Riverside* pumps the boys full of excitement. They run out into their positions faster than usual. Everyone except Albert. Although Albert looked excited when they cheered, Murphy is surprised by how slowly he runs to center field. Something has been different about Albert for the past week or so. Murphy noticed it first at a practice when Haywire ran right past Albert. Haywire can run fast, but no one can run as fast as Albert.

The boys play the best game of the summer. Danny takes a couple of shots on Murphy that are harder than ever. But that only happens when he can get past Jeff, who plays defense like a trooper—he's got his territory covered. Murphy guards the net like he's protecting the Queen—no one's going to get past him without a fight. Even Haywire and the others play like stars.

"The Formidable Four. The Formidable Four!" they cheer each time a play is made.

After practice Murphy repeats the words over and over. He loves the way they sound. There's something about the words that make him feel bigger and better than ever. When he gets home, he looks up the word *formidable* on the computer.

For-mi-da-ble: inspiring respect or wonder because of size, strength or ability

"Formidable," he says to his cat, Mousetrap. "The Formidable Four. That's us, MT. What do you think about that?"

Chapter Three

"Good morning, Riverside students. I hope you are all settling into your new classes. There are a lot of announcements this morning, so everyone listen up." Ms. Clarkson, the principal, has a scratchy voice that makes Murphy cringe, like when Mom stirs cheese sauce in a saucepan with a metal spoon. He ignores the principal until she says, "The first senior boys' soccer tryout will be held on the upper field after the second lunch bell at twelve fifteen. Coach Kennedy wants me to remind you that only boys with full soccer gear will be allowed on the field. That means shoes, shorts, shirts and protection."

Jeez, Murphy cringes, does she have to mention protection right out loud on the announcements like that? Isn't it kind of private? Then he thinks about Albert and the other boys. Murphy has his gear in his backpack, but what about them? At the tribal school, they had only needed a full set of gear when they played a game. How were they supposed to know about Riverside's rules?

After homeroom, Murphy meets Jeff in the hall. "Got your stuff?" he asks. "Did you know about the full set of gear?"

"Yeah, I got it," Jeff says. "And no, I didn't know we needed it. I brought my stuff for PE—didn't even think about needing the whole works for tryouts."

"What about Albert and Danny?" Murphy asks. "What if they don't have their stuff?"

Just then the two other boys race around the corner into the hall.

"What are we gonna do?"

Albert is out of breath. He doubles over, holding his sides.

"We can't even get on the field without a full set of gear!"

Danny is starting to panic.

"Wow, they sure take themselves seriously up here," Murphy says. "They shouldn't tell us we can't try out just because we don't have gear. That's not fair."

"Yeah, it is, Murph. They can do whatever they want. That's why Riverside is so good. They take soccer seriously," Jeff says. He might be right, but he's not being helpful.

"Well, what are we supposed to do now?" Albert says. He's got his wind, and he paces back and forth.

"Go to class, that's what," Jeff says. "We aren't allowed to stand around in the hall."

"But what about tryouts?" Danny says. "What are we going to do?"

"We'll figure it out at recess," Murphy says.

The boys disband and head to class.

Murphy and Danny sit across from each other at the back of the math class. The room is full, but none of the other students look familiar.

Murphy finds it hard to concentrate on the teacher's explanation of fractions when the most important day of the year has just been totally ruined because of one stupid rule. He can't try out if Danny doesn't. They made a deal. They are a pack of four as far as soccer goes—the Formidable Four.

Maybe it's because he's in math class and he's thinking about fractions, but Murphy suddenly wonders, *What if half or a quarter of us don't make it?* He shoves his thoughts into the back of his mind and starts thinking of ways to get Danny and Albert some gear.

"Do you have your shoes?" he whispers to Danny.

"No, but Albert does," Danny replies. "I have shorts and a shirt, but neither of us has protection."

"We have to phone home and get someone to bring some stuff up here," Murphy says.

"Boys. Boys at the back." Mr. Henthorn looks directly at Murphy. "Do you have something to share with the class?"

"No, sir," Murphy says. "Sorry, sir."

The teacher continues talking to the class, and Murphy tries to think of a way to make a call. He's got no money. As far as he knows, none of the other boys bring money to school. The principal already said that students aren't allowed to use the school phone except for emergencies, and probably no one else will think this is an emergency. And anyway, Murphy isn't about to go to the office. That's a place he wants to stay away from.

"We need a phone," he whispers again to Danny.

"Great, who's got one of those?" Danny says. He looks totally discouraged, which is just the way Danny is. If something doesn't work the first time—he quits. It's not a very good characteristic for a great soccer player. Murphy knows that, but there's nothing much he can do about it. Sometimes it's impossible to get Danny to think positive, no matter how hard Murphy tries.

"They don't let us bring cell phones to school. Now what are we supposed to do?" Danny hisses through his teeth. "This is messed up."

Mr. Henthorn stops writing on the chalkboard and faces the class.

"Did someone say something?" he asks.

A few kids snicker.

"I might as well forget the team," Danny says without paying any attention to the teacher. "This place is too stupid."

"Excuse me," Mr. Henthorn says. "If you boys don't stop talking, I'll have to separate you."

Murphy throws Danny a look that says, *Be quiet.* He waits until the teacher turns and begins to write on the board again and then whispers, "I'll find a phone somehow."

The girl at the desk in front of Murphy's has been looking across at Danny and turning her head sideways so she can hear what Murphy is saying. Before Mr. Henthorn finishes writing, she slips a note onto Murphy's desk.

I have a cell phone. You can use it at recess if we make sure no teachers catch us.
Molly

Murphy turns the paper over and writes:

Thank you.
Murphy

He passes it forward. She scribbles something and sneaks it back to him.

Meet me at the Region Street entrance as soon as the recess bell rings.
Molly

Murphy folds the paper and puts it in his pocket.

"No problem," he whispers to Danny. "It's all good."

Danny frowns. He doesn't know what just happened, but he doesn't interrupt the class again. Murphy makes a plan: he'll call Mom at the Band Office, where she works, and ask her to go home from work and get his old shoes and a couple of extra jockstraps. She can bring them up to the school at lunch. The old shoes will fit Danny, and no one will have to root around at Danny's and Albert's places. Mom will do it. Murphy's sure of it. She's as excited as any of them about the boys getting on the team.

When the recess bell rings, Murphy tells Danny about Molly's phone and his plan.

"Go tell Albert that I'll get all the gear we need for everyone. As long as Albert has his own shoes, we can make do with stuff I have around the house."

Murphy's shoes will never fit Albert's big feet, and he isn't sure whether his jockstrap will fit him either. Albert stands head and shoulders taller than Murphy. But if it means he can practice, Albert will just have to suck it up.

Danny takes off, and Murphy heads to the front entrance, where the girl from math class is waiting.

"My name's Molly," she says with a laugh. "But I guess you know that already. And your name's Murphy. I knew that before you told me. My dad told me that you and your mom moved back to the reserve last year. They used to be an item, you know." She stops talking long enough for Murphy to wonder what she means. "Your mom and my dad—at least that's what Dad says. Sounds pretty funny, eh? An item. Dad and I have seen you before, but I can't believe we haven't met each other until now. We live in town. Down by the arena. We just moved there from over the other side of the river."

"Really?" Murphy says. He's not quite sure how to respond, so he says, "Like you say, I'm Murphy," which sounds pretty dumb.

"Oh, sorry," Molly says. "I talk a lot."

You sure are right about that, Murphy says to himself. He thinks about a few other things he could say, but it's hard for him to find a space in Molly's constant flow of words.

"Here." She hands him her cell phone. "Go around the side of the building and make sure no one sees you. They take your phone and call your parents if you get caught. That happened to me a few times. Dad's threatened to close my account."

Murphy can't imagine Mom ever paying for a cell phone account for him.

Mom is okay with picking up the gear and delivering it to the school by the second lunch bell at 12:15. It turns out that Molly knows a lot about Mom, stuff Murphy has never heard about. Apparently when they were teenagers, his mom broke her dad Richard's heart when she dumped him. Richard moved away and married "The Blond Lady," as Molly calls her mother. She left the two of them before Molly had time to get to know her.

"I don't even know what she looks like, other than that she's blond like me. Dad doesn't have even one picture. At least that's what he says. Apparently she lives in New Brunswick somewhere. I'll find her one day," Molly says. "Dad says if I look in the mirror and concentrate on my eyes, and lips that I'll see Mom in there somewhere. That's a pretty lame way to see your mom, don't you think?"

"Yeah," Murphy says when she stops to take a breath. "Pictures are all I get to see of my dad.

Although Mom says I've got his ears and middle toes. Oh, and his light hair and pale skin."

Molly laughs. It's more of a giggle than a laugh, and Murphy realizes he hasn't had a girl for a friend since he lived in town.

"Does that mean your dad has big ears?" she asks.

"What are you trying to say?" Murphy frowns and pretends to be insulted.

"I'm saying you don't have little ears."

The two of them walk around the school looking for the boys, but they can't find them. Murphy tells Molly about the soccer team, the tryouts and the Formidable Four.

"We're the best thing to come from the tribal school since Uncle Rudy," Murphy says, trying not to sound too high on himself.

"I know him," Molly says. "He's a friend of my dad's."

Murphy struts in front of Molly, "We're the fantastic Formidable Four from the Long Inlet Tribal School," he says, beginning to feel comfortable.

"You don't look First Nations," she says.

"Yeah?" he says. "Well, neither do you."

Chapter Four

"Where's Albert?" Murphy asks when Danny and Jeff arrive at his locker.

"He's trying to fit into your jockstrap," Danny says with a laugh.

"Hey, it's not funny," Murphy says. "At least he won't miss the tryout."

On the way up to the field, Albert walks behind the others.

"What's up with you?" Danny says. "Having trouble with that little jockstrap?"

"Naw, it's okay. This place stinks," Albert says. "I can't believe they make us wear full gear just for tryouts."

"Get over it," Jeff says. "We're gonna be on the team. That's the point, isn't it?"

"Yeah," Danny says, and he turns to high-five Albert. "We're the Formidable Four."

Albert ignores Danny and turns his back on his three friends. The rest of the boys who have come for tryouts are standing halfway down the field. They are close enough that Murphy can see every one of the players. There are a lot of them—tall ones, short ones, heavy ones, skinny ones. It's hard to say just from looking who's good and who's not. All he knows for sure is that Riverside won the British Columbia Middle School Championship last year, and he's starting to feel a little nervous.

The four boys stand in a tight huddle. Now that they are getting a good look at the other Riverside players, they all seem worried. If only Uncle Rudy was here.

"Hey, guys," Jeff says. "Don't forget we only have one rule."

Danny slaps Albert's back.

"One rule, cousin," he says.

"And what's that one rule?" Murphy tries to sound like Uncle Rudy.

The boys look at Albert.

"Give 'er all you got!" he says halfheartedly.

The whistle blows.

"Over here, boys." The coach hails them with his arms. "Welcome to the Riverside soccer tryouts. I'm Coach Kennedy. And these are my scouts, Miss Hansen and Mr. Paul." He gestures at two young teachers standing beside him.

Everyone gathers around.

"We're going to have five games over the next two weeks. I'm going to count you off one-two, one-two to make teams. We're going to play fifteen-minute halves. My scouts and I are going to watch you—closely.

"We'll get together at the end of the two weeks and decide among the three of us who gets on the team. No one is assured a spot. Players from last year have to show they are still interested—no shoo-ins, no slackers, no bad attitudes. Now let's go: one-two, one-two…"

The boys shuffle around, trying to position themselves so they will get on the same team. Danny and Murphy end up on one team and Albert and Jeff are on the other.

"Ones at that end and twos at the other," Coach Kennedy hollers. "Hold off a minute! I forgot. Keepers! Over here."

Murphy runs over to the coach. Two other boys join him. One is as big as Albert and looks old enough to be in high school. The other one is small like Haywire. At first Murphy figures that the big boy is going to be his toughest competition. But Murphy can tell that the smaller boy is the one with the confidence—and a confident keeper can be a good keeper, no matter what his size.

"Bingo," Coach Kennedy says to the big boy, "I want you to my left in net and you—what's your name?"

"Murphy."

"Okay, Murphy, you're in net on the right. Ahmed, you will sit out to start. I'll get Mr. Paul to sub you in later."

Murphy only makes one save before Ahmed replaces him. While he's on the sidelines, he studies the players. He makes mental notes on how they kick, which ones are lefties, heavy shooters, fast runners, good ball handlers. It's hard to keep track of which boy is which. The only ones he remembers are Albert and Danny and Jeff.

In the summer it had seemed easy. The Formidable Four were going to be the best players Riverside had ever seen—as simple as that. Now, standing on the sidelines, Murphy knows it's not going to be easy at all. The four of them are good, but so are a lot of the other boys.

"Come on, you guys," he says under his breath. "Good isn't enough. We have to be great."

It's hard worrying about the three of them as well as himself. But they've all got to make the team; that's all there is to it. They are the Formidable Four. It will be a first. Uncle Rudy will be so proud. Murphy can't even think about one or two of the boys not making the team.

Jeff is playing well. He's steady, and he's dependable; the coach will see that. Like Uncle Rudy says, a defensemen has got to be reliable, and Jeff is showing that's exactly what he is. Danny also looks good. But he's running faster than Albert, and that confuses Murphy.

"Bingo, you're out," Mr. Paul hollers and then points at Murphy. "You're in."

Murphy gets into the net just in time to face Albert coming down center field. He's got the ball in control, like it's tied to his foot. It's a beautiful thing to see. When he enters the defensive zone, Jeff challenges him.

Go get him, Jeff.

But no, Jeff backs off.

What's he doing?

From where Murphy is standing, it looks like Jeff just lets Albert go by. Albert heads toward Murphy. He's not running fast, but when Albert meets a goalie, it's scary, even if he's only walking. Murphy takes his position. Albert draws his foot back and then releases a shot.

Murphy braces himself, expecting a hard hit. He's ready for pain. But it's not a shot like Albert usually lets loose. The ball flies straight at Murphy. It's weak and soft, like a shot off Haywire's shoe.

"Nice save, Murphy," Jeff calls.

"Thanks," Murphy calls back.

Albert doesn't look at Murphy. He turns and walks toward center field. Murphy kicks the ball over his head and the play continues.

The last play worries Murphy—right from how Albert got past Jeff so easily to how slowly he was running and how little power there was in his shot. It wasn't a bad play, but it wasn't Albert.

Danny and Jeff perform better than ever. There is no doubt from the game today that the coach will notice them. But Albert! The coach will never know how good he is if he keeps playing like this. Murphy can't believe it. He didn't think it would be Albert he'd be worrying about. It doesn't make any sense.

"Good play, good play, Murphy."

A girl's voice interrupts his thinking.

"What are you doing here?" he says when he sees Molly standing behind the net.

"Watching you and your friends," she says. "The Formidable Four. I'm cheering you on so you'll all get on the team. You're all good. I hope you get to stay on the field long enough for the coaches to see you make some saves."

"Yeah," Murphy says. "Me too."

"What do you think so far?" she says.

I think you should shut up. Just then the ball comes out of nowhere, up into the left corner. He leaps, hands out, without thinking. His left side moves as fast as his right side. The tips of his fingers snag the ball, and he yanks it into his belly and falls.

"What a save!" Molly screams.

Coach Kennedy hollers, "Great save!"

Jeff and Danny are jumping like idiots. Albert raises his hand high-five style and turns around toward center field.

"You can't talk to me while I'm playing," Murphy snaps at Molly.

"Sorry for living," she snaps back. "You made a great save."

"Yeah, but it was a fluke," he says. "I almost missed it."

The truth is that Murphy has just found out that his left side is as good as his right side as long as he's not thinking about it. And that feels good.

"Okay, I'll just leave then," Molly says.

"No, just don't talk to me when I'm in goal," Murphy says. "That's all I'm saying."

Molly hangs around until the end of the game and then walks back to the school with the boys.

"You guys are totally going to make the team," she says.

"Who are you?" Albert asks.

"I'm the one who made it possible for you to play today. It was my cell phone that Murphy used to call his mom."

"And that makes you an expert on who gets on the team?" Albert says.

"You guys are sure edgy. I'm just trying to help. I want you guys to get on the team," she says.

"What's it to you?" Danny says, but he's looking at her as if to say, *What's a white girl doing hanging with us?*

Molly knows what Danny means, and she's not put off one bit.

"I might be blond," she says, "but my dad is from the reserve as well. He lived there a long time ago. We live in town now. I think I'm related to Albert. I don't know for sure."

"You aren't related to me." Albert sounds annoyed. But it's not Molly he should be worried about, it's his playing.

"How do you know?" she says. "I'm going to ask my dad. Albert Adams, right?"

"Whatever," Albert says. He walks ahead without looking back.

"What's with him?" Jeff asks. "He's usually a grump, but not that bad."

"Yeah…," Murphy starts and then stops. He's just about to say that he doesn't think Albert played up to his ability during practice, but he decides against it. He remembers what Uncle Rudy said about the power of positive thinking. If the Formidable Four are going to make the team, they have to support each other—no negative talk.

Chapter Five

The next couple of tryouts are pretty much the same as the first. Murphy makes a few more outstanding saves that get everyone on the sidelines shouting and hollering. And not just Molly, who doesn't miss a practice. She learned fast not to interrupt Murphy when he's playing soccer, or—just as importantly—when he's on the sidelines studying the players. Molly talks a lot, but she knows when to be quiet too.

After the last practice of the first week, the four boys and Molly walk back to the school together.

"Are you feeling okay, Albert?" Molly asks.

"Yeah," he snaps. "Why'd you ask that?"

"I'm just worried about you," she says. "That's all."

"And who are you to be worried about me?" he says, walking ahead. "That's just what I need. Some little freak girl worrying about me."

"I'm just concerned," she says. "And I'm not just some freak girl. We're related. Dad says. Not close, but from way back our families—"

Albert interrupts. "Concerned, concerned. The girl is concerned," he says, mocking Molly. Then he throws her an angry look. "Concerned about what? Are you concerned that I'm not eating enough for breakfast?"

"Why are you so mad at me?"

It's hard to say whether Molly is going to cry or whether she is getting angry. Murphy doesn't know her well enough to judge, but he doesn't want to see either.

"Yeah, well, I'm not into hearing stupid remarks about how I'm playing soccer. *Are you feeling okay? You think I don't get what you're saying? You're just a stupid girl. Why don't you leave us alone?"* Albert's voice is loud. "Why don't you all just leave me alone?" he shouts over his shoulder. He turns and runs to the school ahead of the rest of them.

What really bothers Murphy is that Albert doesn't run like he usually does. He runs slowly, kind of dragging his feet. Murphy has never seen him run like that before. They all watch him, and no one says a word.

Molly finally breaks the silence.

"He looks like he's not feeling very well, that's all," she says. "I wasn't trying to insult him."

Danny says, "Can't a guy have a bad day and not have to explain himself? I mean, who are you to criticize him?"

"I wasn't criticizing him," Molly argues.

Jeff and Murphy look at each other. Murphy waits, because it looks like Jeff is going to say something.

Better him than me. I don't want to say anything about Albert.

"She's not criticizing him, Danny. You know that. She's worried. And I have to say, I'm worried," Jeff says.

"What are you worried about?" Danny voice rises as he glares at Jeff. "Has Molly got you on Albert's back too?"

"That's not it," Jeff says, "and you know it."

"I know what?"

"You know Albert's not playing the way he usually does."

Although Murphy feels sort of glad that Jeff has finally said what Murphy has been thinking, the words themselves make him feel bad—really bad. Murphy had thought there was something different about the way Albert was playing ever since the game in the summer when he let off a weak shot right at Murphy. But when Jeff says the words, Murphy really starts to worry that what he has been seeing in Albert lately is real. Up until now, he has hoped that it is just a figment of his imagination.

"He's just not used to playing with these freaks up here at Riverside. I'm like that too," Danny says.

"No, you're not, Danny," Molly pipes up. "You are playing awesome. You're going to be on the team for sure."

Even though Molly compliments him, Danny's now as mad at her as Albert is.

"We're all going to be on the team," he barks. He waits for a moment and then says, "Why don't you all just shut up? There's nothing wrong with the way Albert's playing, okay? He's better than all these stupid kids."

Murphy knows he should say something. It isn't Molly's fault that Danny's mad. And he agrees completely with what Jeff said. But he can't figure it out. It doesn't look like Albert is trying. He's sloppy and slow. He's not being accurate. There is no power in his shots. Once in a while he looks great, but most of the time he hardly even looks average. It just isn't like Albert. And now he's mad. He not excited about the team. What has happened to the dreams of the Formidable Four?

During the afternoon, Murphy thinks about the soccer team. He thinks about Albert and the plans the boys had made. There is one rule: *Give 'er all you've got.* Now he wonders what will happen if one of the boys decides not to give 'er all he's got. What if one of them really doesn't want to make the team? What if it's Albert who gives up on their dream?

After school, Albert gets on the bus after the other boys. There's an empty seat next to Danny, but Albert sits up at the front by himself.

"What's wrong with him?" Jeff asks.

Murphy says, "I don't know. He's acting totally weird."

"He just hates this school," Danny says. "He told me that the other day. He says he wishes he was still at the tribal school."

"Yeah, well, that's no reason to wreck all the plans. We're the Formidable Four. We gotta make the team. All of us together. It's not fun anymore. I'm so worried about Albert that I can't even play a good game," Jeff says.

"Same with me," Murphy says. "I want to let his shots in just so he can get a goal."

"So what are we going to do?" Danny says. He keeps his voice low to make sure Albert doesn't hear what they are talking about.

Jeff shrugs his shoulders. "I want to kick his butt," he says.

"That's not going to work," Danny replies. "He's already mad at us. He'll just get worse."

"I know what we should do," Murphy says. "Let's get Uncle Rudy to come to tryouts on Friday. He knows how to encourage and kick butt at the same time."

The other boys agree. Of course, Uncle Rudy's what Albert needs. And it's not just Albert who's having trouble adjusting to Riverside. Danny and Jeff and Murphy agree: they are all feeling a little stressed. Getting on the team isn't as much fun as they thought it would be. Some of the other boys are good— really good.

Chapter Six

Mom's reading a book when Murphy arrives home. Mousetrap is curled up on Mom's lap, purring. His thick white coat looks a little grubbier than it used to when they lived in town, but the sight of the two of them makes Murphy feel good. Their place is comfortable—a real Mom, Murphy and Mousetrap kind of place. It's just a basement suite, no doubt about that. It's got some issues. Blankets divide the rooms instead of doors. It doesn't have a lot of windows. But Mom has a way of making a space into a home. The place is full of blankets and pillows and carpets, and when the boys come over, they say it's their favorite house on the whole reserve, even though it started out as an empty basement.

"There's something wrong with Albert," Murphy blurts out as soon as he opens the door.

"Wow, son," Mom says. "Hello to you too."

"Sorry," he says. "Hello, Mom. I'm worried about Albert."

Mom listens as Murphy tells her about the game in the summer—the first time Murphy realized that Albert wasn't playing the way he used to. He explains how Albert's game got worse at the end of the summer and now it has become really obvious at tryouts that something is wrong.

"At first I thought that it was just because we were with other players—ones we'd never played with before," he explains. "I thought maybe Albert was scared and couldn't show his stuff against boys he didn't know. I figured he'd loosen up after a game or two."

Murphy gets himself a plate of crackers and cheese, a glass of milk and an apple, and settles into his favorite chair.

"But he didn't. Then I got worried that maybe he wasn't as good as I thought he was. I got thinking that maybe all of us were just kidding ourselves.

Maybe we're all just bad players. But Jeff and Danny are playing excellent. And every game, I get lots of cheers. I know Coach Kennedy likes me."

"So what's wrong with the way Albert plays?" Mom asks. "I mean, exactly what does he look like?"

Murphy describes how slowly Albert runs and how sloppy his shots have become.

"It's not like him, Mom," he says. "He acting like he doesn't even care. Like he's doing it deliberately. Like he doesn't even want to be on the team. Like he could care less about the Formidable Four."

"That can't be it. But I did hear from his mom that he doesn't like the school," Mom says. "It's all Carmel can do to get him on the bus in the morning. He says he wants to quit and do his schoolwork at home. So maybe that's it."

"It's not that bad up there," Murphy says. "There's a million kids compared to the tribal school. And he's not the biggest guy anymore. You should see Bingo. He's the other keeper that's trying out for the team. He's almost as big as Coach Kennedy."

"Albert probably feels out of place," Mom says. "Give him some time. He'll figure it out."

"He doesn't have any time. There are only two more tryouts, and if he doesn't play hard, he won't be picked for the team. Then what will happen to the Formidable Four?"

"Has he played *that* badly?"

"I don't know if he's played *that* bad. But he sure hasn't played that *good*."

"Maybe you other boys should head up to the field and have a short game before supper. Give him a boost."

"I think we should get Uncle Rudy to come to practice on Friday. He'll kick Albert's butt and give him a boost. What do you think?

"Good idea. He works in town. He might be able to get to your game at lunch."

Murphy phones Jeff and then Danny. They decide that Murphy should be the one to phone Uncle Rudy and tell him about Albert. They have no doubt that with him at practice, they'll all do better.

Uncle Rudy agrees.

"Twelve fifteen, Friday. Riverside Middle School. The upper field. I'll be there, Nephew," he says. "And don't worry about a thing. I remember being totally freaked out about the big school. It affects some kids that way, Murphy. It'll take Albert some time."

"But, Uncle…," Murphy starts.

"I hear you. I hear you," Uncle Rudy butts in. "He doesn't have any time. Friday's the day. I'll be there."

"Thank you. Thank you so much, Uncle."

Murphy is relieved. It seems like his plan is the answer. There is no way that Albert will slack off when Uncle Rudy's around. Not a chance.

"No problem. The Formidable Four will make the team. That's the plan. All four of you will *give 'er all you've got*. That's the rule."

"Thanks again."

"Say hi to your mom for me. Later."

Murphy phones Danny and then Jeff. "He's going to be there," he says.

"Awesome," Jeff says. "I sort of know how Albert feels. It's kind of scary having all that competition."

"I do too," Murphy says. "We'll all do better with Uncle on the sidelines."

Murphy is sure of it. It will be like old times. The four of them—showing up all the other boys on the field. Coach Kennedy won't be able to turn them down.

"Did you say that Albert looks tired all the time?" Mom asks when he gets off the phone.

"Sometimes, I guess. He's not running as fast as he used to."

"And his shots? Did you say they were weak?"

"Yeah. What about it?"

"Nothing. I was just wondering."

"Wondering what?"

"Nothing. I'm sure he'll play really well for Rudy."

Chapter Seven

"Where's Albert?" Danny asks at the bus stop Friday morning.

"He's coming," Jeff says. "I talked to him last night."

"Then how come he's not here? The bus is on Beach Road already. I saw it turning the corner a few minutes ago," Murphy says.

When the bus pulls up to the stop, Albert is nowhere to be seen. The boys get on along with half a dozen other Riverside students.

"Morning, boys," Uncle Spencer, the bus driver, says. "It's your big day today, I hear. The last day you get to impress the coach. You boys are going to make us proud."

"Yeah, Uncle," Jeff says. "But Albert's not here."

"Anyone seen him?" Danny says loudly when he gets onto the bus. "Anyone seen Albert this morning?"

"No."

"I haven't."

"Me neither."

The other kids all shake their heads.

"We passed his house, and I didn't see his mom's car in the driveway. Must mean she's already gone somewhere," Shawntay says. She lives a few houses away from Albert.

Uncle Spencer waits for a while, hoping to see Albert run around the corner and hop onto the bus.

"I can't go looking for him now," Uncle Spencer says. "The rest of you will be late for school. But I'll check it out when I get back home after I drop you off. I'll make sure he gets to school somehow."

"Thanks, Uncle Spence," Jeff says.

The boys sit near the middle of the bus. They don't say anything, but they can hear the other kids talking.

"Albert better show up," one girl says.

"Yeah, no kidding," another girl replies. "He's the best player we've got."

"He's got the best chance at making the team."

"He'll make it anyway. Even if he doesn't show up. He's that good."

Murphy doesn't mind hearing what the kids are saying. He knows Albert's the best. At least, Albert has always been the best in the past. What the other kids on the bus don't know is that their soccer hero is at risk of losing a position on the team. He needs to do more than show up to get on the team. He needs to be awesome.

Molly meets the boys in front of the school at recess.

"I saw Albert in the office this morning with his mother," she says. "They were talking to the principal."

"No way," Danny says. "What do you think is going on?"

Just then Albert comes out the front doors.

"You're here," Jeff hollers. He slaps Albert on the back. "You had us all worried that you'd miss the game at lunch."

"Of course not," Albert says and slaps him back. "We're the Formidable Four. Do you think I'd let you down?"

"Never," Danny says. "There's only one rule: *Give 'er all you've got.*"

"That's right," Albert replies. "And we're going to do it."

Murphy is relieved. Albert is here. He sounds excited about the final tryout. At least the words that he says sound excited. But there is something about the way Albert is talking that unsettles Murphy. It might be that since Murphy became a goalie, he's learned to watch the *game*—the whole game. He's learned to watch the smallest movements. He's learned to anticipate what a player is going to do before he does it. It's in the way he dips his shoulders, the way he leans left or right. It's the little things—the not-so-obvious movements—that Murphy watches for. That's why Murphy makes a good goalie. He doesn't miss a thing.

Right now Jeff and Danny are hearing only what Albert is saying, but they are missing what Murphy can see—the unspoken stuff. There's definitely something Albert's not saying, although Murphy can't figure it out. But whatever it is, it threatens to mess up the tryouts, and that makes Murphy nervous.

"Sure good you're here," Molly says. "We were going to send out a search crew to look for you."

"Where were you?" Jeff asks.

Albert's face loses its smile. "You don't need to send no spies after me," he snarls. "It's none of your business where I was. I'm here, aren't I?"

Murphy's confused. An erratic player is the hardest to judge. Murphy can't tell what Albert's going to do next. He seemed excited at first, and then not one minute later, he's angry. Can he really hate Riverside that much?

"I'm at this lousy school, and there's nothing I can do about it," he grumbles.

"But, hey," Murphy says, "it's going to be a whole different story once we all get onto the team. Just like we've been planning all summer—the Formidable Four. The first time Riverside has ever seen anything like it."

"We are going to do it," Danny says. "At lunch, suited up, ready to give 'er all we've got."

Murphy thinks about telling Albert that Uncle Rudy is coming to the tryout, but he decides it will be better to surprise him. The boys high-five each other when the bell rings. Everyone high-fives Molly, except for Albert.

"We are going to do it," they say to one another.

Jeff punches the air and says, "This is our last chance to show our stuff. We are the tribal-school talent."

Uncle Rudy's already at the field when the boys arrive at lunch. He's talking to Coach Kennedy.

"Hey, guys," Uncle Rudy says. "I'm sorry I didn't show up before…I wanted to be here, but I've been too busy at work. We've got one more chance, and we've got one rule. What is it?"

"Give 'er all you've got," they say in unison.

Coach Kennedy calls out the names on the starting lineup. Murphy is on the side. He stands next to Uncle Rudy and says, "Thanks for coming. We all need you, especially Albert."

Uncle Rudy watches the players. His eyes bounce from Jeff to Danny to Albert. Murphy watches as well. Jeff and Danny are playing like all-stars. If they don't make the team, it will be because the coach is blind. But Albert isn't playing well at all—no better than mediocre. Murphy knows what mediocre means.

Me-di-o-cre: adequate but not very good

Mediocre is one of the words Uncle Rudy uses.

"Listen to the word," he says. "It sounds like it needs improvement. A mediocre player is the sort of player that gets overlooked. You don't want to be mediocre. It means you're not giving all you've got. It means you've got some bad attitude happening."

Mediocre is exactly how Albert is playing. He's no better than the other boys on the field. Maybe not even as good as most of them. And if the coach is watching out for attitude, then Albert's in trouble. It's not only Danny, Jeff and Murphy that can see he's got a bad attitude. He shows it on the field.

"You're on, Murphy," Mr. Paul hollers. "Show your stuff, kid."

Murphy likes the way Mr. Paul talks to him. He compliments every play he makes. Miss Hansen is really supportive too. Murphy doesn't know what Albert has to complain about.

Murphy turns toward the game just in time to see Albert chest-butt a tall skinny boy. The boy stumbles and then charges at Albert, who then says something Murphy can't hear.

Coach Kennedy blows the whistle and shouts, "Albert!"

Albert walks away from the coach.

"Hey, young man, when I call your name, don't walk away," Coach Kennedy says. Albert turns around. "Now what did you say to Leroy?"

"Nothing," Albert shouts and tosses Leroy a nasty look. "I didn't say nothing, okay?"

But the coach must have heard him swear. "You watch your mouth," Coach Kennedy says and blows the whistle. "I don't want to hear any of those words on my field."

The game resumes. In a nice smooth play, Albert steals the ball from another player and heads toward Murphy.

Good job, Albert, Murphy thinks. Like old times.

Albert starts out quickly, but slows down as he nears the net. He's holding his side when he lets the ball go. It's a smart shot. He fakes Murphy out, shoots it to his left side, but it's slow enough that Murphy has plenty of time to grab the ball. His left side is not as slow as it used to be, and Albert's shot is not as fast. But Murphy lets the ball fly right through his fingers.

Albert raises his hands and trots back to center field. No one cheers—not for Albert and not for Murphy.

In a few minutes, Coach Kennedy pulls Albert off the field and subs in another boy. Albert ignores Uncle Rudy and stands near the end of the field. Things are not turning out the way Murphy had wanted.

Something has gone desperately wrong. And he doesn't know what it is or how to fix it.

Coach Kennedy blows the whistle.

"Tryouts are over, boys," he calls. "You all did well. If I could pick every one of you, I would, but as you can see the numbers are too high. Riverside Strikers is a prestigious team. Not everyone gets to play. If you are in grade seven, don't worry. You can try again next year. But any of you who don't make it—don't stop trying. Just put your shirt back on and come out again next season."

Danny, Jeff and Murphy gather around Uncle Rudy. He shakes their hands and says, "Good playing, guys. You are all strong contenders."

"But…," Danny says, looking toward Albert, who's standing by himself.

"I know," Uncle Rudy says. "I'll talk to him."

"I'll be meeting with my scouts on the weekend," Coach Kennedy shouts. "I'll post the team roster after school on Monday on the announcement board next to the office."

Chapter Eight

On the weekend, when Murphy first phones Albert, his mom says he's not home. The next time he phones, she says Albert doesn't want to talk to anyone. Murphy phones Jeff and Danny to see if they've talked to Albert.

"Yeah," Jeff says. "The first couple of times, I couldn't get him. The third time, he came to the phone, but he didn't say much."

Danny says that when he asked Albert to come over, Albert said he was playing video games and didn't want to go anywhere. "It was like he didn't want to see me. Weird. He's just acting weird."

"So what do you think is up with Albert?" Murphy asks the other boys when they come to his place on Sunday evening to talk. "What has happened to him?"

"All I can figure is that he hates Riverside," Danny says. "He wishes he was still at the tribal school."

"I guess so," Murphy says. "But he loves soccer, and Riverside will be a lot better when we all get on the team."

"We're his friends," Jeff says. "Why won't he talk to us? Why is he mad at us? What have we got to do with Riverside?"

"Yeah," Danny says. "What's his problem?"

"I sure wish I knew," Murphy says.

"Well, he's starting to get me mad," Danny says. "We worked hard for the team. The Formidable Four—we had a plan. Now look at him. He thinks that he can just wreck the whole thing."

"I don't think he wants to wreck it for us," Jeff says. "Do you, Murph?"

"Yeah, he thinks this is all about him, and it's not," Danny says. "We all gotta go to Riverside. I'd rather be in the tribal school too. But it's going to be great if we make the team."

"*When* we make the team," Murphy corrects him.

"Do you really think we'll make it?" Jeff says.

"I'm not as confident as I was before," Danny says. "Especially after seeing Albert play. I'm freaking out. Maybe we aren't as good as we thought we were."

"Same with me. I'm thinking just like you," Jeff says. "We had a big plan, and now it's all gone wrong. Maybe we were just dreaming. Maybe it's all just a big stupid mistake. Maybe none of us has a chance."

"Yeah, but what about Uncle Rudy? He wouldn't lead us on. He knows soccer, and he'd tell us if he thought we didn't have a chance," Murphy says.

⚽ ⚽ ⚽

"Welcome back to school, all you Riversiders," Principal Clarkson says over the PA on Monday morning. "Especially the soccer contenders. The starting lineup will be posted on the bulletin board by the office this afternoon. You can check out the list after final bell. The lunch monitors…"

Murphy stops listening once the soccer announcement is over. Albert wasn't on the bus again this morning. And even without worrying about Albert, Murphy has lost his confidence. Getting on the team seems like an impossible task. From what Murphy can tell, Bingo is a darn good goalie, and Coach Kennedy already knows him. Even the small guy, Ahmed, who isn't much smaller than Murphy, is pretty good. That means Murphy has only a one-in-three chance of making the starting lineup. The numbers don't make him feel very good.

Then there's the problem of Albert. All of a sudden, the Formidable Four seems like a really bad idea. Instead of the four boys supporting each other, they are just worrying about what it will be like if they don't all make the team.

"Looks like Albert's not coming," Jeff says when the boys and Molly meet out in front of the school at lunch.

"Maybe he'll still get here," Molly says. "He was late on Friday."

"It's not like him," Danny says. "His mom never drives him to school. Albert never misses a chance to play soccer. Something's really messed up."

"Do you want to use my phone to call his mom?" Molly asks Murphy. "Do you think he's forgotten about the selection?"

"Are you kidding?" he says.

Free time at lunch seems like a couple of hours. Time goes so slowly in math and technology classes that it feels like the afternoon will never end. Murphy can't decide whether he's excited or terrified when the after-school bell rings. He leaves the classroom slowly. The list won't be going anywhere. It can wait. He shuffles his feet on the way to his locker. He tidies up some papers and books and tosses a few old apples and bananas into the garbage before he gets his jacket and backpack.

There's a bunch of boys crowding around the bulletin board in the foyer. Jeff and Danny stand off to the side, waiting for a space near the list.

"Hey, Murph," Jeff says as soon as he appears. "I think your name's on the list. The big goalie stomped out of here like he was going to hit something."

Murphy swallows hard. He doesn't want to get excited without seeing for himself. He needs to see his name with his own two eyes.

"Did you guys make it?" Molly asks when she arrives. "Tell me, tell me. I can hardly wait."

"We don't know yet," Murphy says.

"We can't get close to the list," Danny says. "These guys need to learn how to read. They haven't moved since we got here."

Murphy can hear names being called, but he doesn't recognize any of them.

"What are you waiting for?" Molly says. She pushes her way into the crowd until she's standing in front of the list. "Jeffrey Sam, Daniel Waters and Murphy James," she calls out. "Starting lineup!"

Jeff and Danny high-five. They turn and high-five Murphy. His stomach rumbles like there's a whole set of marbles tumbling around inside.

"Way to go!" Molly screams when she emerges from the huddle. "You're on the team. You guys are great."

When a few boys move away from the list, Murphy inches his way through the crowd to the front. His eyes zoom over the names until he sees *Murphy James* printed in black and white. He puts his face closer to the list. Plain as day, right there in front of him, no mistakes, it says: *Murphy James, Starting Keeper*. He looks away from the list and then checks it again: *Murphy James, Starting Keeper*. Again he looks:

Murphy James, Starting Keeper. His eyes are not playing tricks on him. There's no doubt about it. He's on the team.

He checks the list again. It is just as Molly said: Jeffrey Sam and Daniel Waters and Murphy James are the only three names Murphy recognizes. He looks at the top of the list. Albert Adams? His name should be at the top. But Albert Adams is not on the list.

He didn't make the team.

Jeff made the team. Danny made the team. Murphy made the team. Albert did not make the team. *Three-quarters*, Murphy thinks. *Only three-quarters of us made it.*

It takes a little while for the fact to sink into Murphy's head.

Ever since the boys started practicing in the summer and planning to make it onto the Riverside Strikers, only one guy was a shoo-in: Albert. Everyone *knew* he would make the team. Danny, Jeff and Murphy were hopefuls. They had a good chance, but not like Albert. There isn't a grade-seven player in the entire region who is better than him. Murphy checks the list again.

By now Danny and Jeff have made it to the front of the crowd. Both boys check for their names. Then their eyes flick up to the top of the list. Bobby Bristol is the first name. There are no names starting with *A*. No Albert. No Adams.

"Wow," Jeff says as he walks away from the bulletin board. "That's hard to believe."

"It sure is," Danny says. "I thought I would be the one who didn't make it. Not Albert."

"Or me," Murphy says. "No wonder the big keeper is stomping around. I can't really believe I made it and he didn't."

"Albert didn't make the team," Jeff says, his jaw slack.

"There goes the Formidable Four. We can't be the Formidable Three," Murphy says. "It doesn't sound any good. It's just not right."

"Come on, you guys," Molly says. "You did awesome."

"Who's going to phone and tell him?" Jeff asks, ignoring her. "I sure don't want to be the one."

"Me neither," Murphy says. "But somebody has to."

On the way home, Murphy is excited and surprised at the same time. He's on the team. It's not that he thought he *couldn't* make it. But deep down inside, he hadn't been sure. With Bingo being so big and Ahmed being so confident, Murphy had thought his chances weren't that good. But numbers aside, he hadn't imagined what it would feel like to actually read his name on the list—*Murphy James, Starting Keeper.*

Chapter Nine

When Mom gets home, she opens the door and says, "Okay, son, tell me how you did. Was Murphy James's name on the list?"

"Sure was," Murphy says. "MT," he says to his cat when it walks in behind Mom, "you're looking at the starting keeper for the Riverside Strikers. Yes, that's right, my little puddy cat, you are looking at the grade-seven player who beat out two grade-eight players in the lineup. Big Bingo is playing fill-in for Murphy James. He's pretty mad."

Mousetrap curls his body around Murphy's legs and lies down on his feet.

"Congratulations, son," Mom says. "I knew you'd do it."

She gives Murphy a big hug and then flops on the sofa. "Now tell me more. What about the other guys? How did they do?"

"Danny and Jeff made the team," Murphy says. Then, and he's not sure why, he has trouble telling Mom about Albert. He stops talking. He doesn't want to say the words.

"And…," she says, obviously expecting him to continue, "what about Albert?"

"He didn't make the team, Mom," Murphy says. His eyes start to burn. He turns away from her and picks up Mousetrap. "Albert didn't get on the starting lineup, MT. Can you believe it?"

"Well, that's ridiculous," Mom says, throwing her hands up in the air. "Who were the people choosing the team? What do they have against Albert?"

"It's not like that, Mom," Murphy says. "Remember what I said about the way he was playing? I've been worried all week. Well…I've been worried for longer than that. He just hasn't been playing like Albert."

Mom calms down a little. "But Albert is better than most boys, even when he's playing at half speed," she says. "Heck, he's better with one hand tied behind his back. He's the best player since Uncle Rudy."

"That's kind of how he was playing—with one hand tied behind his back and at half speed," Murphy says. He decides not to tell Mom about the fight Albert almost got into or the swearing or the bad attitude he's been tossing around the field.

Murphy tries hard to hold back his tears.

"I don't understand," Mom says. "But I remember now. I didn't like the way it sounded when you said his shots were weak and he wasn't running as fast as he used to."

She gets up to start cooking supper.

"What did he say when he didn't make the team?" she asks.

"He wasn't at school today," Murphy says.

"Well, that doesn't make sense either," she says. "He was looking forward to this as much as the rest of you boys."

"We were going to be the Formidable Four. The first time ever that four players from the tribal school had a chance at making the starting lineup for the Riverside Strikers."

"There's something wrong," Mom says.

"Danny says Albert hates middle school and wishes he was still in the tribal school."

"Do you think that's it?"

"I don't know. I guess. He sure sounds like he hates the school."

"But everyone is worried about moving to a bigger school where there are older kids. He didn't have to destroy his dreams. He wouldn't have played badly because of that." She hesitates. "Or would he?"

She scrunches up her nose like she does when she can't figure something out. She opens the fridge door and pulls out the milk and cheese.

"What is going on with that boy?" she says over her shoulder. "Albert shouldn't be that worried about the bigger school. He's big enough to be in grade eight."

Mom's right, Murphy thinks. Albert's bigger than Jeff or Danny, and he's a whole lot bigger than Murphy. But lately Albert looks smaller—like he's been losing weight.

In bed that night, Murphy hears Mom on the phone. She's talking quietly, so he has to listen closely to understand what she's saying.

"Kelsey, have you talked to Carmel lately?"

There is a long pause. Jeff's mom must have a lot to say.

"Really? Who said that?…Oh no…When will they find out for sure?…That's really too bad. I wondered what was going on with Albert…Yeah. Murphy was saying the same thing…They must be really worried about him…No kidding…Let me know when you find out anything…Yeah, I agree. I don't think I'll tell Murphy either. Maybe we should wait until we know something definite before we say anything to the boys…Jeff sounds like Murphy. Happy about making the team, but really disappointed for Albert."

As soon as Mom disconnects from Jeff's mom, she dials again. Something's desperately wrong, and Murphy can count on Mom to find out what it is.

"Tsina? Yeah, did you hear about Albert?"

Mom takes the phone outside the back door. She shuts it behind her so Murphy can't hear what she says.

What about Albert?

Why doesn't Mom want me to listen?

Why won't she come and tell me? Albert's my friend, not hers.

Murphy's brain won't stop thinking, and none of his thoughts make him feel good. He has too many questions that he can't answer.

By the time Mom comes back into the house, Murphy is sleepy. He decides to wait until the morning to find out what's going on.

Chapter Ten

"Mom." Murphy taps Mom on the shoulder. It's only 5:30 AM, but he can't sleep. "What's wrong with Albert?"

She turns over lazily and says, "What time is it?"

"It's five thirty," he says. "I've been awake since four. I need to know what's wrong with Albert."

"What do you mean, what's wrong with him?" she says, as if she doesn't know anything.

"I heard you last night on the phone. And anyway, it's obvious. Something is wrong."

She slides over and makes room for Murphy to sit beside her on the bed.

"I don't know exactly," she says.

"But you know *something*. You know more than I do."

"I'd rather wait to talk about it—until we hear more. I don't know enough, Murph. It will just worry you."

"Mom, I'm worried already. What do you think I am? A little kid that can't figure anything out?"

"It's just that…"

"Albert's my friend, Mom. I want to know."

"No one knows for sure yet. He has been having tests."

"Tests for what?"

"They think he has leukemia. They'll get the final test back today. Then we'll know for sure."

"What's leukemia?" Murphy asks. He's never heard the word before, and it sounds pretty scary.

"It's a blood condition," she says.

"What kind of blood condition?"

"Not a good one. But it can be cured. That's really all I know, honey. I'll phone around and see if I can find out more about it."

Murphy gets off Mom's bed. He needs to know more. He can't wait until later. He's got too many questions, and they are burning a hole in his head.

He hates waiting—the longer he has to wait, the bigger the hole will get.

He heads back behind the blanket that makes up the wall of his bedroom. He turns on his computer and types the word *Lukemia* into Google. *Do you mean: Leukemia?* it asks him.

He clicks the Wikipedia entry.

Leukemia or leukaemia (Greek leukos, "white"; aima, "blood") is a cancer of the blood or bone marrow and is characterized by an abnormal proliferation (multiplication) of blood cells, usually white blood cells (leukocytes).

The word *cancer* makes Murphy's stomach tighten and the saliva in his mouth dry up. That's the same thing Grandpa had. Cancer. At least that's what Mom says about her father. He died before Murphy was born. Leukemia is a scary word, but it's not as bad as cancer. Murphy's eyes scan the page as he scrolls farther down.

Symptoms: fever, chills, weakness, fatigue, bone pain, joint pain, weight loss…

None of it sounds any good. But Albert's only twelve years old. Why would he get cancer? Murphy scrolls up and down until he finds the causes:

1. *Natural or artificial ionizing radiation*
2. *Certain kinds of chemicals*
3. *Some viruses*
4. *Genetic predispositions*

Only the part about chemicals makes sense. Murphy's seen programs on TV about pollution, and he knows it has something to do with chemicals, and somehow it's all got something to do with cancer.

He googles *radiation*.

Radiation: as in physics, is energy in the form of waves or moving subatomic particles

Murphy doesn't have a clue what subatomic particles are, never mind how they could give Albert cancer.

He googles *genetic predispositions*.

A genetic predisposition is a genetic effect that influences the phenotype of an organism

Murphy doesn't understand most of the words, but he's heard of genetics. Mom told him about it. It's the thing that makes you a certain way because your mom or dad are that way. Like Mom said: She's short. Dad's short. So Murphy's going to be short.

"Don't bother dreaming about being tall," she told him. "It's genetics. You're going to be short."

Maybe someone in Albert's family had leukemia, and that means Albert's going to have it, which is a totally bad deal for Albert, if that's what runs in his family.

By the time Mom gets up, Murphy knows a lot more about leukemia than he did before, but he still has a lot of questions.

The biggest question of all is: how will Albert get rid of it? Murphy couldn't understand a word in the *Treatment* section of the Wikipedia entry. There were drugs with names so long that Murphy couldn't even begin to pronounce them.

"How long will it take for Albert to get rid of the leukemia?" Murphy asks as soon as Mom gets out of the bathroom.

"I don't know, Murphy," she says. She looks like she hasn't slept very well. "Like I said, I'll look into it today."

"It sounds like there's lots of drugs to take. And that it takes a long time. And that…" Murphy doesn't want to say any more. Nothing he read sounded any good—even the stuff he could understand didn't make him feel very optimistic about Albert.

"Where'd you get your information?" she asks.

"The Internet," he says.

"You can't always depend on the information you get on the Internet, Murph," she says. "You know that."

Murphy has one more question—the biggest one of all. It's a question he doesn't want to ask. It's a question he doesn't even want to think about. He sits at the table and pours milk on his cereal. He has to ask. Even if the answer is yes.

"Mom."

"Yeah, Murph."

"It says leukemia might be caused by a virus."

"Yeah?"

"Does that mean I can catch it from Albert?"

"Oh, honey." Mom grabs Murphy's shoulders with both hands. "No, no, no. You can't catch it. Is that what you think?"

"No," he says. "It's just that…"

He's quiet for a few moments.

"Do I have to go to school today, Mom?" Murphy asks. "I'd rather go and see Albert."

"Albert will be busy today. From what Tsina said, he's going to the doctor today to get the final test results and talk about treatment."

"Shouldn't he have a friend with him?"

"We'll see later this afternoon. Maybe you can call him then."

Chapter Eleven

That evening Mom has the whole story. At least, she has the story that Jeff's mom got from Danny's mom, who spoke to Albert's grandma.

Albert's sickness started back in the spring, just after the Easter Tournament. First he started complaining that his bones hurt. Then, in the summer, he began to feel tired a lot of the time. That's when his attitude went from bad to worse. He wasn't just grumpy sometimes, he was grumpy all the time. Finally, around the first week of school, his mom took him to the doctor. It didn't take them very long—they did a few blood tests, and now they are sure he has leukemia.

For now Albert has to take a lot of drugs. Then, after a while, he will have to go to Vancouver to a big hospital. No one knows for sure how long he will need to stay or how many times he will need to go there. Albert's family's pretty worried about that part of it. His mom has other kids and a job, which only leaves his grandma to go down to Vancouver to look after him in the hospital.

When Mom's finished describing Albert's condition, Murphy gives him a call.

"Sorry, Murphy," Albert's mom says. "Albert says he doesn't want to talk to anyone."

Murphy tries to phone the next day and the next. But it's the same every time: Albert doesn't want to talk. Finally, when he calls, she says, "He's coming, Murphy, just hang on for a minute." So Murphy waits and waits until the line is disconnected.

Albert doesn't ignore only Murphy. He won't talk to anyone. And to make matters worse, he doesn't come to school all week or show up at the field on the weekend.

"We have to do something about Albert," Jeff says on Monday morning. "We can't just leave him alone and forget about him."

Danny says, "He doesn't want to see us. We can't force him. So what are *we* supposed to do?"

When they get to school, Molly is waiting at the bus stop.

"Where's Albert?" she asks.

"He's sick. Really sick," Murphy says.

"I don't even want to see him," Danny says. "When I phoned him the other night, he was shouting at his mom, 'Tell Dummy to quit phoning me.'"

Molly says, "Did he really say that?"

"Yeah," Danny says. "And he's making me mad. I'm sorry he's sick, but I'm not sticking around so he can call me junk like that."

"But Danny," Molly says, pointing her finger, "you have to understand how Albert feels. He's your friend, and he must feel awful." She sounds like someone's mom.

"Oh, great. He calls *me* names, and *I* have to understand how *he* feels," Danny says. "I don't think that's how a guy's supposed to treat his friend."

Danny's attitude doesn't seem right to Murphy, but he sort of understands how Danny feels. Just because Albert's sick doesn't mean he can treat Danny badly.

"Anyway, Molly," Danny carries on. "Albert's all we've been thinking about lately. Is he going to make the team? Oh, poor Albert, he didn't make the team.

Now he's sick, and it's still all about Albert. Is it just me, or is anyone else tired of worrying about Albert?"

"Wow, Danny, that's not very nice," Murphy says. "I'm not tired of worrying about Albert. I'm just glad it's not me who's sick."

"Yeah, well, you're not sick, and neither am I. So why can't we just forget about all this?" Danny says. "We made the team. He didn't. Now he's wrecking it for us. It's not fair."

"Am I hearing you right, Danny?" Molly gasps. "Is that what you really think?"

"Duh," Danny says. "I just said it, didn't I? What do you think? That I'm lying to you?"

Danny runs ahead toward the school, leaving Murphy, Molly and Jeff walking together silently to the front door.

❂ ❂ ❂

At lunch when the boys walk up the hill to the field for soccer practice, they have their heads down. No one says a word.

Nothing has worked out the way it was planned. First Albert doesn't make the team. Now he's sick, and it doesn't help that Danny has such a bad attitude. The first two games were okay, but nothing like Murphy had expected. Playing for the Riverside Strikers isn't any fun at all. It's the end of the Formidable Four. Everything is a disaster.

"Hey, guys, tonight's a big game," Molly says when she catches up to them. "They say the Tempo Lake Tigers are going to be our biggest threat this year. They have a whole lot of returning players."

"They won't even come close," Jeff says.

"Oh yeah?" Danny says. "They probably think we're a bunch of losers. Riverside sucks."

Murphy tries to think of something to say, but what's the point? When Danny gets this way, there's not much anyone can do about it. But Danny's wrong. Riverside doesn't suck. They've won both their games so far. The first game was a slaughter—11–0 for Riverside. It was as if the other team didn't even show up. Even Jeff got a goal. The second game was tough, but it ended with Riverside up 2–1 with a great goal from Leroy.

Danny's shoulders slump as he walks onto the field.

"I don't even know why I bother playing on the team," Danny mumbles as he walks away. "Without Albert, we're going nowhere."

Molly stands silently beside Murphy for a few moments.

"We have to do something, Murphy," she finally says. "We can't just let everything fall apart. This is your dream."

"*Was* my dream," Murphy says, trying to remember how excited he used to be when he thought about being on the Riverside Strikers. That's when he thought that if he could make the team, then everything else in the world would be perfect. Now he isn't even excited or proud. The truth is, even though Murphy is on the team, he has never felt as unhappy as he does today.

"No, no, no, Murphy," Molly says, standing with her hands on her hips. Murphy is amazed at how much she reminds him of his mom. "Playing for the Riverside Strikers IS your dream. And it's Danny's dream and Jeff's dream too. We gotta do something."

"What can we do?" Murphy asks. "We can't make Albert better. We can't get the Formidable Four back together. We can't change Danny's attitude. Once he gets like that, he stays like that."

Molly raises the palms of her hands to the sides of her head. "You make me crazy," she says. "Just go and play. I'll think of something."

After practice, Danny and Jeff run ahead. Molly and Murphy take their time walking down the hill.

"The all-schools intramural tournament is coming up in a few weeks, isn't it?" Molly says.

"Yeah, I think so," he says. "In a month or something like that."

"It's going to be held at Riverside this year, right? Teams are going to come from all over the place."

Murphy doesn't respond.

"It would be a good time to have a fundraiser."

"A fundraiser for what?"

"Think about it. Albert must be scared. First he can't play soccer like he used to, and then he doesn't make it on the team. Then he finds out he's sick, and now he has to go to Vancouver to have treatment— and his family can't afford to make the trip over and over again. And they don't even know how long he'll have to be there. Wouldn't you be scared?

"Yeah. No kidding. I heard his grandma's going to stay with him."

"Maybe, but it is going to cost a lot of money just to get his mom and the kids to travel back and forth."

"There's nothing we can do about that."

"Come on, Murphy. We can't change the fact that Albert's sick. And we can't get him back on the team, at least not right away. But we can do something to help him feel better and maybe not so scared."

"I can't think of anything."

"You're as bad as Danny."

"Don't say that."

"Okay, but think of it this way. The whole thing sucks, but there is something we can do. We can't make it go away, but we can make it better."

Murphy curls his shoulders up to his ears. Molly is so optimistic. Maybe she's got a point, but right now he doesn't think there's much a couple of kids can do to improve the situation.

"First of all we need to get excited about the team. You guys should be happy. Right?" Molly pokes Murphy in the shoulder. "Right? Come on, Murphy, agree with me. You know I'm right."

"Okay, okay, you're right," he protests. "We have to get excited about the team."

"Then we have to get some money together so that Albert's family can afford to get back and forth to Vancouver and have a good Christmas." She stops and waits for Murphy to respond.

"Okay, okay, you're right again. We have to raise some money."

"Then we have to encourage Albert so that he becomes the best cancer patient in the whole world. People get better from leukemia, you know. But Dad says people heal better when they are happy. And from the sounds of it, Albert is not very happy right now."

The bell rings before Murphy has time to say anything else, but he knows Molly's right. It seems like Albert has given up, and that's not going to help anything.

Maybe I've given up too, he thinks. Maybe Molly's right: everything doesn't have to be completely hopeless.

In fact, once Murphy starts thinking about Molly's plans, he starts feeling better.

Chapter Twelve

After school the boys are at the field when Molly arrives.

"Come on, you guys," she says when she gets close to where they are standing. "Play like you're playing for Albert. Get 'er done."

The words sound funny coming from Molly. Jeff throws her a sideways look, and Danny scowls.

Murphy puts his hand on Danny's shoulder and says without very much enthusiasm, "Yeah, guys, let's go and get 'er done."

Danny pushes Murphy's hand away and heads onto the field.

"We're the Riverside Strikers," Jeff says, trying to sound excited. "Let's get out there and play like a team."

"Way to go," Molly says. "You're not the Formidable Four. You're the starting lineup for the Strikers."

She's right, Murphy thinks. We're not the Formidable Four anymore. We're the Riverside Strikers. We're part of the team. And that's a good thing.

He looks at the boys on his team one by one. Up until then, he hadn't really thought much about any of them other than how they kicked or ran or passed the ball.

"Way to go, Danny!" Murphy shouts when Danny takes a great shot and almost scores.

"Good goal, Reza!"

"You show 'em, Walker!"

When Murphy cheers for the other boys, he feels good. He's not one of the Formidable Four. He is a Riverside Striker. They are a team.

It's an easy game for him. Jeff and the other Striker defenders play so well, there aren't many serious Tempo shots on goal. Murphy only makes a few great saves and a couple of blocks, and he gets a shutout. The Strikers take down the Tempo Lake Tigers handily, 3–0.

"You guys are great. You guys are great," Molly cheers when the game is over. "The Riverside Strikers sure showed those guys who's the best. Good team, good team, good team."

She jumps up and down and throws a high five at Murphy and Jeff, but Danny turns to go before she can congratulate him.

"Hold on, Danny, I need a word with you," Coach Kennedy calls to him as he walks away. "Wait a minute," he says as an afterthought, "I'd like to talk to Jeff and Murphy as well. Can you fellows hold on a minute?"

The other players head toward the school, leaving the three boys and Molly behind with Coach Kennedy. He tosses each one of them a few balls and water bottles that have been left on the field.

"How's it going with you boys?" he asks.

"Not bad," Jeff says.

"How do you like playing for the Strikers?"

"Good," Jeff says. He nods his head. "Yeah, it's good."

"I'm surprised that you boys aren't more enthusiastic. I had heard good things about the effort you put in this summer for the team. I heard we were going to get some mighty excited players from the tribal school."

"So what are you saying?" Danny snaps. "That we're not playing good enough for you?"

"Hey, buddy, not so fast," Coach Kennedy says. "I'm the coach, and my job is to take care of my players. I'm just wondering if you're making the transition to Riverside okay. I know it can be hard for some kids. You guys look a little down, that's all."

"Nothing wrong," Danny mumbles with his head down.

"We're fine," Jeff says. "We're all good."

Molly, who has been standing off to the side, joins the boys.

"That's good," Coach Kennedy says. "Because if you have any concerns, you can come and talk to me anytime."

"They have a concern," Molly pipes in.

Danny straightens up and says, "Who are you to be talking for me?"

"I'm your friend," she says. "And I'm Albert's friend too."

"Albert?" Coach Kennedy frowns.

"He's the guy that didn't make the team," Danny snarls. "The guy you overlooked. The guy who wasn't good enough for you."

Coach Kennedy looks confused.

"Danny," Jeff says, trying to calm him down. "Lay off, bro."

"Albert? You wanna know about Albert? He's the best player of us all." Danny glares at the coach. "He's just a guy from the reserve who happens to be better than any other player on this dumb team." Danny squints to hold back his tears. "He's the reason I play soccer. He's the one who showed me all my moves, ever since I was a little kid. If it weren't for him, I wouldn't be on this team."

"I know who you are talking about," Coach Kennedy says. "But…"

"Oh, now you remember him." Danny's almost shouting by now. "Maybe if you didn't keep him off the team, maybe he wouldn't have quit school and maybe he wouldn't be sick right now."

Danny chucks the soccer ball he is holding at Coach Kennedy, catching him off guard and hitting him on his shoulder. He turns and races toward the school.

Molly kicks the ball to Jeff.

"Coach," she says. "I'm so sorry. He didn't mean to do it. Really, he didn't."

Coach Kennedy stumbles a bit and then sits down on the bag of balls. He motions with his hands for the boys to sit beside him.

"You too," he says to Molly. He tosses her a ball to sit on.

"I think I'm missing something here," he says. "Please, someone tell me what is going on."

If Murphy thought things couldn't get any worse, he just found out he was mistaken. He can't believe his eyes. His best friend shouted at the coach and hit him with a ball. Jeff's mouth hangs open, and Murphy's knees are shaking.

"You see, Coach Kennedy…," Molly begins before either boy speaks. She tells him how hard the boys practiced all summer, how they called themselves the Formidable Four and how Albert was the head of the gang, the best player, the inspiration, the soccer hero for all the younger boys at the tribal school.

She tells him that his playing got worse and worse until he didn't make the team. She tells him that Danny got mad, Murphy got worried and Jeff got scared. No one knew what to do. She says it wasn't until a few weeks ago that they found out that Albert has leukemia, and most of the teachers don't even know yet. Now, for some reason, Danny blames the coach. Finally Molly stops talking and takes a big breath.

"Nothing has gone right, Coach Kennedy. It was so good at the start, and then things started to go wrong. Now it's just one big disaster," Murphy says.

"I hear you," he says. "I wish someone had told me earlier. I would have brought Albert onside and used him on the sidelines even if he couldn't play."

"Well, we only just found out that he's sick," Jeff says. "And no one really likes to talk about it."

They all stand up and start walking back to the school.

"I'll talk to Danny," Coach says. "But you kids are going to have to help me. It looks like he thinks I'm the bad guy."

"And maybe you could help us," Molly says. "In a few weeks, Albert has to start going to Vancouver for treatment. His mom can't go with him all the time.

She has to work, and she has two other little kids. We need to raise money to help her travel to be with him and so his grandma can stay with him and to help them out with Christmas. We need to show him that we care about him. We need to get him back to school. There are SO many things we need to do. We have to get started."

"I'll do whatever I can," Coach says.

Chapter Thirteen

Murphy feels better when he thinks about Molly's plan. He figures she's probably right when she says they won't be able to fix some of the major problems, but they can make a difference with other stuff.

Murphy thinks that Molly is one of the most unusual friends he has ever had. It's not because she's a girl. It's because she doesn't ever quit. Nothing stops her. At first that part of Molly was a little hard to take. Jeff and Danny aren't used to her yet. They think she's weird. And Albert doesn't have a clue what to think of her. But now that Murphy's gotten to know her, he likes it that she never gives up. He likes it when she talks. Most of the time, she talks about interesting things. And he likes it that she is so positive—especially right now, because positive is the last thing Murphy has been feeling lately.

In fact, Murphy comes to the conclusion that Molly really is a lot like his mom—she's always coming up with stuff. If there's a problem, Molly has a solution, just like Mom. She's got a positive way of looking at things. She doesn't let trouble get her down—not completely down. That's another thing Murphy likes about her. Maybe it *is* because Molly and Mom are both girls. Murphy thinks for a few seconds that he likes that about Molly too.

"Hey there, MT," Murphy says when he gets home from school. "We won the game. The Riverside Strikers are awesome—the best team in the league—soon to be the best team on the Island."

Mousetrap fluffs up his tail and rubs against Murphy's leg while Murphy pours himself a glass of milk and makes a cheese sandwich.

"Remember when I told you how excited I was about the team?" Murphy drops his cat a piece of bread. "Well, today is the first day that I realized I'm really on the team. I'm not one of the Formidable Four anymore, MT. I'm a Riverside Striker. I'm the keeper of the Riverside Strikers."

Mousetrap always seems to appreciate Murphy's stories. He curls up on his lap and purrs. He keeps one eye open, and that way Murphy knows he's still listening.

Murphy describes the game play by play. By the time he gets to the part where he gets a shutout, Murphy starts to feel the same old excitement coming back—just like he felt in the summer when the Formidable Four were dreaming about being on the team.

"Bobby plays center. He's good, but not as good as Albert. Walker plays defense with Jeff and Taylor in center back…"

"You talking to your cat again, Murphy?" Mom says when she comes in from work.

"Yep," Murphy says. "And he agrees with me. MT says I'm completely right."

"That Mousetrap is a smart cat." Mom throws her jacket and purse on the sofa.

"He's as smart as me," Murphy says. "But he doesn't come up with so many good ideas."

"What good idea did you come up with today?" Mom asks.

"It wasn't exactly me who came up with the ideas," he says. "But I was the first one to agree with them."

"What does that mean?"

"Well, there's this girl at school," Murphy says. "Have I told you about her?"

"How would I know?" Mom says, laughing. "You haven't told me what girl you are talking about."

"Molly."

"No, you haven't told me about Molly."

Murphy wonders for a second or two why he hasn't told Mom about Molly before. And then for another second, he wishes he hadn't mentioned her, but now he doesn't have any choice. He needs to tell Mom about the plans. And anyway, it's not like Molly is a secret—she's his friend.

"Well, Molly's a girl in my math class."

"Okay."

"And Molly says you and her dad were an item when you were in high school," Murphy says. He wishes right away that he had left out the part about Molly's dad.

"An item?" Mom laughs again.

"Yeah, you know, like going out."

"Oh, I see. An item means we were going out. Well, that narrows it down to about three guys. So what is Molly's last name?"

"Jacobs."

"Ooohhh. Yes. I do remember her dad. You could say we were an item. Or you could say he was my first love."

"Let's not talk about your first love, okay?" Jeez, Murphy thinks to himself, the last thing I want to be talking to Mom about is love. "I'm just trying to tell you about Molly."

"I heard that Richard lives in town, but I haven't seen him since we got back."

"Mom, I said I was talking about Molly."

"Right. Sorry, Murph. What about Molly?"

"Do you even remember what we were talking about?"

"Sure, we were talking about Molly."

"No, we were talking about Molly's good idea."

"Right. Now tell me about the good idea."

Murphy fills Mom in about everything, and once they stop talking about love and Molly's dad, it feels good. He hasn't really talked to her for days. He tells her that Albert hasn't been to school and all the boys have been feeling miserable. He tells her that Danny's been downright angry and blames Coach Kennedy for everything, and that up until this afternoon no one cared one bit about the team. He tells her that the whole soccer thing and school thing were turning out bad—really bad.

"That's where Molly comes in," Murphy says, and then he describes how Molly became his friend, how she talked to Coach Kennedy and how she came up with a plan.

"Wow," Mom says. "I like Molly already. You let me know what kind of help I can be. I'll do whatever I can."

⚽ ⚽ ⚽

"I was talking to my dad last night," Molly says the next morning. "He helped me put together a plan. You guys tell me if you think it will work."

"A plan for what?" Danny says. "A plan to mess things up worse than they already are?"

"Danny," she pleads, "don't be so negative."

"And I guess you are going to tell me things aren't negative."

"No, I'm not, but it's nobody's fault. Albert is sick. It's not his fault, and it sure as heck isn't my fault."

"If Coach Kennedy had picked him for the team, Albert would be here at school," Danny insists. "The Formidable Four would still be together. Now look where we're at. We're nothing."

"Coach Kennedy couldn't pick Albert. Not the way he was playing. And even if he had, Albert would still be sick and unable to play," she says.

"He can play," Danny argues. "He's just too embarrassed to come to school because he didn't make the team."

Molly looks at Murphy and then Jeff. They both shrug their shoulders as if to say, *What can we do?*

"Mom says in a few weeks Albert will be going to Vancouver to get his cancer treated," Murphy says.

"He doesn't have cancer," Danny snaps. "He's got leukevia."

"Leukemia," Molly corrects him. "It's a type of cancer."

"No way," Danny cries. "That's not true. That's not what my mom says."

"Danny," Murphy shouts. "Stop it. Stop denying it. None of the rest of us like it either, but Albert's got cancer, and we can't do anything about that."

Jeff butts in, "Yeah, Danny, but we can do something to help him out. If *you* hate thinking about Albert being sick, can you imagine how *he* feels?"

Danny turns and looks at Jeff. "What do you mean we can do something about it?"

Molly says, "That's what Dad and I were talking about. There's a few things that really suck for Albert right now. First, he isn't coming to school. Second, he's not getting to the soccer games. Third, his family doesn't have enough money to travel to Vancouver to be with him while he's in treatment. With Christmas coming, that's double bad. And fourth, he doesn't have any friends anymore, because we've all ditched him."

"We haven't ditched him," Danny says. "He ditched us."

"I know, but no one's been to see him," Molly says. "He's ditching us because he's afraid. And we're letting him ditch us because we're afraid. That's what Dad says is happening."

"Whatever you say," Danny shrugs. "I'm listening."

Molly says, "We should convince him to come back to school, even if he doesn't feel very well. At least for the soccer games. He can hang out with Coach Kennedy. Maybe Albert can help him coach."

"And Mom agrees that we should do a fundraiser to help the family," Murphy says. "She says she'll help."

"Awesome," Molly says. "'Cause that's what Dad says as well."

Danny puckers his brow and says, "I got a question here. What's Albert got to do with you and your dad, anyway?"

"I'm Murphy's friend, and Albert's Murphy's friend, so I'm Albert's friend," she says. "That's how it works. That means I'm your friend too. Even if you don't know it."

Danny frowns and shakes his head. "I guess," he says.

"And one more thing," Murphy says. "While we're talking about changing things up around here, I was thinking about the Formidable Four. It doesn't exist anymore. We're the Riverside Strikers now, and that's even better. It's not just about us. It's about the team. There are lots of guys on the team," Murphy holds up his fingers as if he's counting. "There's Reza, Walker, Bingo, Leroy, Bobby and a bunch more. And when Albert gets better, he'll be part of the team."

"There's Reuben and Troy," Jeff says.

"And that guy named Zeke," Danny adds.

After school the boys decide that everyone shouldn't go to see Albert at once—Jeff and Murphy will go first. They will tell him about Molly's plan and see what he has to say.

Chapter Fourteen

"Let's go to Albert's house right now," Jeff says when the bus stops in front of his house.

"No, I gotta go home first," Murphy says. "I got some stuff to do for Mom. I'll be over in half an hour."

"Okay, meet me here."

When Jeff gets off, Murphy's the only student left on the bus.

"Did you hear about Albert?" the bus driver hollers over his shoulder.

"Yeah, I did," Murphy says. He wanders up to the front.

"What a bad deal that is, eh?" Uncle Spencer says. "How's he doing?"

"I don't know," Murphy says. "I haven't seen him."

"You haven't seen him? No way," Uncle Spencer says. "I thought you boys were his best friends."

"We are," Murphy says, hearing how lame it sounds.

The bus lurches to a stop near Murphy's house. He jumps off the bus.

"I'm going to visit him now," he calls over his shoulder. "I'll let you know how he is tomorrow."

Murphy races into the house, drops his backpack, grabs a banana and runs back out the door to Jeff's house. His chores can wait.

It's been almost two weeks since Murphy's seen Albert—and they are best friends. Molly's dad is right. Murphy was afraid. He still is afraid. He doesn't know what to say. He doesn't know how to act around a sick guy. Cancer, leukemia—it sounds so scary.

☻ ☻ ☻

"What are we going to say to him?" Jeff says when Murphy gets to his house.

Murphy says, "Since when have we ever been worried about what to say to Albert?"

"Since right now," Jeff says. "He's angry, and I don't like Albert when he's angry."

"And he's sick, and I don't know what to say when someone's sick," Murphy admits. "But like Molly's dad says, Albert's afraid, even more afraid than we are."

"Yeah," Jeff says. "But I still don't know what to say to him. I still don't like it when he gets mad."

"Me neither."

The two boys walk past the soccer field to Albert's house. When they get to the door, Jeff knocks lightly. Murphy feels like a bird's flying around in his stomach.

"Jeff? Murphy?" Albert's mom looks surprised. "It's been a long time. Nice to see you."

Her shoulders are slumped. There are folds under her eyes and a deep crease on her forehead that Murphy hasn't noticed before.

"Come in," she says. She sounds uncertain, as if she's not sure whether the boys should be there. Rennie and Louie, Albert's little sister and brother, don't seem to be around, and the house is unusually quiet.

Mrs. Adams shuffles down the hall to Albert's room while the boys stand nervously by the front door.

She says something in a muffled voice.

"I didn't invite them over," Albert says, loudly enough for the boys to hear.

Again his mom speaks. Murphy can tell from her tone that she's trying to convince Albert of something.

"Tell them I don't feel very well," he says rudely.

She says, "You tell them," and then shuts the door hard.

"You probably heard him," she says when she comes back. "I don't know what to do. He won't come out of his bedroom."

"Can we go in to see him?" Murphy asks.

"Sure. But I don't know if he'll be very nice to visit."

Mrs. Adams looks tired and defeated—like she's played a hard game and lost 3–2 in overtime.

"That's okay, Mrs. Adams. We have to try," Jeff says. "We're sorry we didn't come earlier."

"That's okay, boys," she says. "I know it's hard on everyone."

Murphy taps on the door. "Albert? Albert?" he calls. "Can we come in?"

There is no response.

"Hey, Albert, come on, bro," Jeff says. "We're here to visit with you."

It's quiet.

Murphy turns the door handle and opens the door slightly. "You okay with us coming in?" he asks.

Albert sits hunched over on his bed. The sun coming in behind his back makes him look small. When Murphy gets closer, he can see that Albert's skin is pale and his face looks thin.

"Hey, Albert," Jeff says, "What's up with you?"

"A whole lot, as you can see," Albert says. "It's just one big party in here. I'm having a great time. That's why you guys came over, isn't it? To have a great time with Albert."

Murphy takes a deep breath. He's afraid to speak. If he says something nice, Albert's going to snap back. He can't think of anything to say about soccer or school. And he's scared to say anything about Albert's sickness.

Jeff smiles nervously. He looks as uncomfortable as Murphy feels. The room is quiet and still except for the sound of Albert breathing. It sounds like someone blowing up a balloon.

Without thinking too much, Murphy blurts out, "We know you are sick. That must totally suck. It totally sucks for us too, 'cause we miss hanging out with you."

Albert and Jeff look surprised. Even Murphy can't believe he was so straightforward.

"Yeah, I am," Albert says. "And yeah, it does."

Suddenly Murphy feels better. The words had been stuck in his throat, and once they came out, talking wasn't as hard as he thought it would be.

"We really miss you on the soccer team," Jeff says.

Albert swallows hard. "You do?"

"He's not kidding," Murphy says. "It's not the same without you. You were the one who made a goalie out of me."

"Oh yeah, well, this is the end of the game for me," Albert says, squinting to hold back tears.

He can't talk like that, Murphy thinks. He has to be positive, like Molly says. It'll help him feel better.

Jeff and Murphy sit on the bed next to Albert.

"It's not the end of anything," Jeff says.

"What do you know about it?" Albert barks and moves away.

"Nothing," Jeff admits. "I don't know anything about being sick."

"Yeah, well, I'll tell you something about it," Albert's voice is loud now. He sits up straight and looks at the boys through the tears in his eyes. "It stinks.

It stinks like a rotten pig. It's like a great, big freaking black cloud is hanging on top of my head all the time. It never goes away. Sometimes it sinks down so far that I'm smothered. It's all around my face. I can hardly breathe. The cloud comes up my nose, and the stink of it gets stuck in my head. It doesn't lift off. Not even for one minute. It stinks. It just stinks."

Tears spurt out of Albert's eyes.

Murphy's jaw drops. Never in a million years would Murphy have imagined hearing words like that coming from Albert.

"That sounds awful," Jeff says. His eyes are wide and wet with tears.

Albert slumps over and says, "It's never going to go away. Never."

"No, Albert, no," Jeff says. "Never say never. I was looking on the computer and finding out stuff about the sickness you got. You're going to get better, and you'll play soccer again."

"Does it say that on the computer?" Albert snaps. "Does your computer say that Albert Adams's leukemia is going to go away, that Albert is going to go back to school, that Albert is going to play soccer? Does it say that? I want to see where it says that."

"Okay, so it doesn't say those words exactly, but it says that tons of kids get over childhood leukemia."

"Does it also say that some kids don't get over it?" Albert is talking quietly now.

"I don't know about that," Jeff says. "I just want *you* to get better. I read a story on the Internet about a professional football player who had leukemia when he was a kid. He was twelve, just like you. And now he's playing for the Montreal Alouettes."

Murphy says, "That's why we're here, bro. We're here because we're going to help you get better."

"What can *you* do about it?" Albert wipes his eyes and nose on the back of his shirt. "There's nothing you guys can do about it."

"Uh-huh, there is," Jeff says. "We might not be able to cure leukemia, but we can be good medicine. Mom says that friends are the best medicine there is."

"Molly's dad was saying that feeling better has a lot to do with attitude," Murphy says. "And the best medicine for attitude is friends."

"We know you don't have the best attitude some-times, so we're here to help you out with that part." Jeff slaps Albert on the back.

"And one other thing," Murphy says. "We need you on the field whether you're playing or not. Coach Kennedy says you can help him watch the plays and you can—"

"I'm not going to the field," Albert says. "Not unless I can play."

"I think I know how you feel, but you gotta come out anyway," Jeff says. "We want you there. You'll feel better if you get up and—"

"Did you guys know that after this treatment I'm doing now, I gotta go to Vancouver for some other kind of treatment?"

"Yeah," Murphy says. "And we got some ideas about that. Molly wants to do a fundraiser so your mom and the kids can come and see you more often when you and your grandma are in Vancouver."

"We got some great ideas, Albert," Jeff says. "But we need you to help us help you."

Albert shrugs his shoulders and sighs. "Won't do any good," he says and then turns the other way.

"But, Al—," Murphy starts, but before he can say Albert's name, Albert interrupts.

"Don't bother, you guys," he says. "It's no use."

"No, Albert," Murphy says, more determined this time. He knows leukemia is a serious disease, but he'd read on the Internet that there were plenty of treatments. They weren't nice treatments, but they worked. "There's lots of reasons for us to bother."

"I don't want to go to school," Albert says. "I didn't make the team. That's the only thing I wished for, and now look at me."

"Come on, Albert," Murphy pleads. "Just think about it."

"I don't feel like it," Albert says. His voice is louder than before. "Why don't you guys just go now?"

Murphy and Jeff get up, but before they go out the door, Murphy says, "You can feel bad at school just as well as you can feel bad at home."

"Hey, Mrs. A.," Murphy says when they meet her in the kitchen on their way out. "Tell Albert there's practice after school tomorrow. We'd sure love it if he showed up."

Chapter Fifteen

The next day the boys walk slowly up the hill to the field.

"I guess Albert decided not to come," Murphy says.

"Did you really think he'd show?" Jeff asks and then turns toward the parking lot just in time to see Albert slam his mom's car door.

He is out of breath by the time he reaches the boys on the field. Jeff gives him a high five while Murphy and Danny slap his back.

"Good to see you, Albert," Murphy says.

"Really good," the other boys say.

Coach Kennedy has a chair waiting next to the soccer bags.

He blows the whistle and hollers, "Everyone over here for a huddle."

All the players gather together.

"I don't know if all you guys know this fellow," Coach Kennedy says, placing his hand on Albert's shoulder. "His name is Albert Adams. He didn't have enough time earlier in the season to show us how good he is. But I got a call last night from Rudy Richards, Riverside's most famous soccer player, and he told me that he's never seen a grade-seven player better than this guy. The trouble is, Albert's got a nasty disease, and it's going to take some time for him to get better. So when he's feeling well enough, Albert's going to help me with some of my coaching duties. He's going to keep his eye on you players and let me know where he thinks you can improve."

Some of the boys on the team look sideways at Albert as if to say, *Who the heck is he?* Others mumble, "Jeez, sorry to hear it."

Danny speaks up. "Coach Kennedy is right. Albert's better than anyone on this team."

"Rudy told me one more thing," Coach Kennedy says. "He told me that the boys from the tribal school have a cheer, and with their permission I want to use it with the Riverside Strikers."

Albert laughs out loud. It's the first time Murphy's heard him laugh in a long time.

"What do you think, Albert? Can we use it?" Coach Kennedy asks.

"Sure," he says, looking at the other boys. "I guess so. What do you guys think?"

Jeff and Murphy nod.

Danny says, "Really, Albert, do you think it's okay?"

"Hey," Albert says, "I got a call from Uncle Rudy last night, and he said I'm part of the team."

"Well, then," Coach Kennedy says. "Show us how it's done."

The boys put their hands together, make the spokes of a wheel and shout:

> What's our name? Yeah!
> What's our name? Yeah!
> Get 'er done and win the game!
> Goooooo, Strikers!

"Come on," Coach Kennedy says to all the boys. "Let's see if we can make some noise."

The whole team puts their hands into the circle and shouts the cheer. When they are finished, Albert punches the air and says, "Yeah, let's go, Strikers."

Chapter Sixteen

From then on, all the players of the Riverside Strikers and Coach Kennedy huddle at every practice and game and do the cheer.

Albert helps Coach Kennedy sub players in. He watches from the sidelines like he used to watch them on the field. He helps them improve their plays. Especially Danny, who is happy Albert is there to support him. Albert has a good eye for when a player is injured or isn't feeling well. Now that Albert stands on the sidelines, he takes a lot of interest in the players' health. Coach Kennedy loans him his first-aid materials and other books about sports injuries. In fact, since Albert hasn't been feeling well, he has started to like reading. Between Coach Kennedy and Molly, he has all the books he can read.

Molly and her dad, with the help of Murphy and his mom, Danny, Jeff, the other players and their parents, organize a fundraiser. They print posters and hang them on telephone poles and tack them to the notice boards in the school, in town and on the reserve.

ALBERT ADAMS FUNDRAISER
DINNER AND AUCTION
RIVERSIDE MIDDLE SCHOOL
DECEMBER 4
5 PM
Come and enjoy a meal together.
There will be lots of good stuff at the auction
and lots of good music by
Rudy Richards and Arnold Adams.
Funds will be donated to the Adams family
to help with travel expenses to and from
the Children's Hospital.

Albert's mom brings dozens of homemade dinner rolls. Other parents bring spaghetti, lasagna, macaroni and cheese, ravioli. Everyone knows that Albert's favorite food is pasta. Molly and her dad make salads. Mom bakes two cakes and puts them together to make the biggest cake Murphy has ever seen. She decorates it with soccer balls and goalposts to make it look like a soccer field. She writes *Get 'er done* in the middle. Murphy, Jeff and Danny set up the school gym. Coach Kennedy arranges the auction items people have donated. Albert's Uncle Arnold and Uncle Rudy set up their guitars and amplifiers next to the food tables.

By the time Ms. Clarkson welcomes everyone to the event, there are almost two hundred people sitting at the tables. Before they eat, Albert's grandmother stands up. She beats a hand drum and sings a prayer song. Then she thanks everyone for supporting her family and especially Albert.

"You are all medicine for my grandson. Good medicine. The good feelings in this room tonight will help him to heal. In Vancouver the doctors will give Albert treatment. I will go with him, but it is you who have given us what we need to be healthy. You are our medicine. Albert is a winning soccer player. Now he has a different kind of game to play. And he cannot win this game without his team." She spreads her hands out. "You are his team. Albert will be back. He will play with the boys again."

When everyone has finished eating and after Coach Kennedy auctions all the items, Mom and Molly's dad lay a blanket on the floor. While Uncle Rudy and Albert's uncle sing a song they wrote for Albert, one by one people walk up to the blanket and drop money into it. Some people drop coins, some drop five- or ten-dollar bills. Some people even drop twenty dollars or fifty dollars. The Formidable Four stand at the corners of the blanket surrounded by all the rest of the Riverside Strikers. When the song is over, the boys fold the blanket and take it into the kitchen to count the money—$2,200—more than enough.

Before anyone gets up to go home, Murphy calls Coach Kennedy and the boys together in a huddle in the center of the gym. He puts his hand into the middle. The rest of them follow, making a circle with spokes. They holler:

> What's our name? Yeah!
> What's our name? Yeah!
> Get 'er done and win the game!
> Goooooo, Albert.

Acknowledgments

Thanks to the young people in my family and the ones who read my books. You continue to inspire me to tell stories and write them down. Thanks to the wonderful Andrew Wooldridge and Bob Tyrrell at Orca Books, who make books for young people an art form and work so hard to get books and kids together. Thank you both for the privilege of publishing with your great company. And, of course, to my editor (and wonderful author) Sarah Harvey—thank you, thank you for keeping me on track.

Sylvia Olsen is the author of two previous Orca Young Readers as well as two Orca Soundings. She lives in North Saanich near Victoria, British Columbia, with her partner Tom, and Jude, their very beautiful and energetic Australian shepherd.